Michael Hague's
TREASURY OF
CHRISTMAS CAROLS

by Michael Hague *and* Kathleen Hague

STERLING CHILDREN'S BOOKS
New York

Jingle Bells

Dashing through the snow,
in a one-horse open sleigh,

O'er the fields we go,
laughing all the way.

Bells on bobtail ring,
making spirits bright.

Oh, what fun it is to sing
a sleighing song tonight!

Oh! Jingle Bells! Jingle Bells!
Jingle all the way!

Oh, what fun it is to ride
in a one-horse open sleigh, hey!

Jingle bells! Jingle bells!
Jingle all the way!

Oh, what fun it is to ride
in a one-horse open sleigh, hey!

Deck the Halls

Deck the halls with boughs of holly,
Fa la la la la, la la la la.

'Tis the season to be jolly,
Fa la la la la, la la la la.

Don we now our gay apparel,
Fa la la la la, la la la la.

Troll the ancient Yuletide carol,
Fa la la la la, la la la la.

See the blazing Yule before us,
Fa la la la la, la la la la.

Strike the harp and join the chorus,
Fa la la la la, la la la la.

Follow me in merry measure,
Fa la la la la, la la la la.

While I tell of Yuletide treasure,
Fa la la la la, la la la la.

Fast away the old year passes,
Fa la la la la, la la la la.

Hail the new, ye lads and lasses,
Fa la la la la, la la la la.

Sing we joyous all together,
Fa la la la la, la la la la.

Heedless of the winds and weather,
Fa la la la la, la la la la!

O Christmas Tree

O Christmas Tree, O Christmas Tree,
Forever green your branches!

O Christmas Tree, O Christmas Tree,
Forever green your branches!

How bright in summer's sun they glow,
How warm they shine in winter's snow.

O Christmas Tree, O Christmas Tree,
forever green your branches!

O Christmas Tree, O Christmas Tree,
You give us so much pleasure.

O Christmas Tree, O Christmas Tree,
You give us so much pleasure.

A grove of fir trees standing near
Brings joy and beauty through the year.

O Christmas Tree, O Christmas Tree,
You give us so much pleasure.

O Christmas Tree, O Christmas Tree,
Your faith is strong and steadfast.

O Christmas Tree, O Christmas Tree,
Your faith is strong and steadfast.

It teaches us fidelity
And courage through adversity.

O Christmas Tree,

O Christmas Tree,

Your faith is strong

and steadfast.

We Wish You a Merry Christmas

We wish you a merry Christmas,
we wish you a merry Christmas,
we wish you a merry Christmas
and a Happy New Year!

Glad tidings we bring
to you and your kin,

Glad tidings for Christmas
and a happy New Year!

Please bring us some figgy pudding,
Please bring us some figgy pudding,

Please bring us some figgy pudding,
and bring it right now!

We won't go until we get some,

We won't go until we get some,

We won't go until we get some,
so bring it right now!

We wish you a merry Christmas,
we wish you a merry Christmas,

we wish you a
Merry Christmas
and a
Happy New Year!

Notes about the Songs

Jingle Bells

On cold November nights in the mid-nineteenth century in Massachusetts, spirited sleigh races often would take place. While watching one of them, James Lord Pierpont was inspired to write a song, which he called "One Horse Open Sleigh." This tune is now called "Jingle Bells," and it is sung while faces are smiling and silver bells are ringing. But the song originally wasn't written with Christmas in mind; it was meant to be sung at Thanksgiving.

"Jingle Bells" is said to have first been performed at a children's Thanksgiving show. The mothers, fathers, brothers, and sisters of the singing children loved the song. The tune was very catchy and bright. Everyone begged for it to be sung again at the Christmas show. From then on, "Jingle Bells" would always be sung at Christmastime and whenever there would be snow on the ground and merry people at hand to sing a tune.

Deck the Halls

A long time ago, carols were thought of as dance tunes, not songs. One of them that we now know as "Deck the Halls" was a very old melody from Wales. It was composed in the mid-eighteenth century as a harp dancing tune by John Parry Ddall.

The song originally had no words. But during dances, singers would compete for the best rhymes to the shuffles, turns, and steps to the tune. They would make up the words as they went along. The lyrics were first written down by the poet John Ceiriog Hughes.

The English words to "Deck the Halls" we know today include "follow me in merry measure," which refers to dancing a measure. A measure is another word for dance.

"Deck the Halls" remains a popular Christmastime song, although it was originally meant to be sung on New Year's Day.

O Christmas Tree

The German "O Tannenbaum," known in English as "O Christmas Tree," is an old folk tune that has been sung in many different versions. The most popular tune was composed in the early nineteenth century by Ernst Anschütz, an organist and teacher.

The song is about the most well-known symbol of Christmas: the big, green, decorated holiday tree. The original Christmas tree was a fir tree (in German: *Tannenbaum*). It was brought in from the frosty outside and adorned with lights and ornaments. Often it was placed near a fireplace or in a central point of the house—as it still is.

A Christmas tree makes the holiday season merry and brings family and friends together in decorating it. With lights glowing and special decorations hanging from the branches, it invites the spirit of the holiday into every home. Having a Christmas tree around results in smiles of happiness and inspires good tidings for a delightful holiday.

We Wish You a Merry Christmas

Each year in England, on long winter nights, carolers often would gather and sing to the gentlemen and gentlewomen in the town. One tune, "We Wish You a Merry Christmas," was sung aloud in exchange for Christmas treats. A favorite one was figgy pudding, a white Christmas pudding filled with figs.

The composer of the tune is not known. Still, singing the song at holidays remains a tradition.

"We Wish You a Merry Christmas" was one of the first songs to wish people a happy New Year. It can be sung on both Christmas and New Year's Day.

A NOTE ABOUT THE ILLUSTRATOR

Michael Hague was born in Los Angeles in 1948. When he was growing up, he was greatly influenced by comic books, animation work of the Disney Studios, Japanese printmakers Hiroshige and Hokusai, and turn-of-the-century illustrators Arthur Rackham, W. Heath Robinson, N. C. Wyeth, and Howard Pyle.

Michael developed his artistic skills at the Los Angeles Art Center College of Design. He later spent years designing greeting cards for companies, first in Kansas City, Missouri, and then in Colorado Springs, Colorado. He has remained in the Rocky Mountains area with his wife, Kathleen, who has written several books for children.

In 1980 Michael became a freelance illustrator. His first major illustrated book, *The Wind in the Willows*, ushered in a renaissance of illustrated children's books. Since then, more than a hundred other books with Michael Hague illustrations have followed, including classics such as *Peter Pan* and the *Velveteen Rabbit*.

In early 2001, to adapt to developments in the rapidly changing world of publishing and illustrating, he began to learn how to paint on the computer. Since then, he has created many books that have utilized and synthesized his old-school skills, developed over the course of decades, with newly acquired drafting abilities on the computer. Among them are a graphic novel, *In the Small*, and *White Christmas*, a fantasy interpretation of the familiar Christmas song.

"Each new book is an exciting beginning," he says. "As far as I can see, the future looks bright for new and exciting projects."

STERLING CHILDREN'S BOOKS
New York
An Imprint of Sterling Publishing
387 Park Avenue South

STERLING CHILDREN'S BOOKS and the distinctive Sterling Children's Books logo are registered trademarks of Sterling Publishing Co., Inc.

Library of Congress Cataloging-in-Publication Data Available

Lot#:
2 4 6 8 10 9 7 5 3 1
04/11

Published by Sterling Publishing Co., Inc.
387 Park Avenue South, New York, NY 10016
This book was originally published in 1990 in four separate volumes (*Jingle Bells,*
We Wish You a Merry Christmas, Deck the Halls, O Christmas Tree)
by Henry Holt & Company
Editorial matter © 2011 by Sterling Publishing Co. Inc.
© 1990 and 1991 by Michael Hague
Distributed in Canada by Sterling Publishing
c/o Canadian Manda Group, 165 Dufferin Street
Toronto, Ontario, Canada M6K 3H6
Distributed in the United Kingdom by GMC Distribution Services
Castle Place, 166 High Street, Lewes, East Sussex, England BN7 1XU
Distributed in Australia by Capricorn Link (Australia) Pty. Ltd.
P.O. Box 704, Windsor, NSW 2756, Australia

Printed in China
All rights reserved.

Sterling ISBN 978-1-4027-7812-4

For information about custom editions, special sales, premium and
corporate purchases, please contact Sterling Special Sales
Department at 800-805-5489 or specialsales@sterlingpublishing.com.

Designed by Liz Trovato